God
MADE EVERYTHING

SEEDLiNGS
BOOKS TO GROW ON

Chariot Books™
David C. Cook Publishing Co.

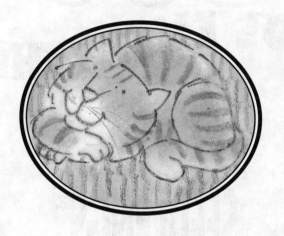

This book about creation belongs to

Shaquan Raheem Drayton

From

Virginia Ford (Grandma)

With your child, praise God for His creation—
from the vast expanse of sky to the smallest
fish in the brook. But praise Him most of all for
making you. Encourage your child to name
more things God made that you see every day—
a favorite pet, a flower that grows in your
window box, or the caterpillar crawling
along the sidewalk.

Chariot Books™ is an imprint of David C. Cook Publishing Co.
David C. Cook Publishing Co., Elgin, Illinois 60120
David C. Cook Publishing Co., Weston, Ontario
Nova Distribution Ltd., Newton Abbot, England

GOD MADE EVERYTHING
© 1990 David C. Cook Publishing Co., Elgin, IL

Written by Karen Bigler
Illustrated by Bartholomew
Cover designed by Helen Lannis
First Printing Revised Edition, 1994
Printed in the United States of America
98 97 96 95 94   5 4 3 2 1
ISBN 0-7814-1539-X

Originally titled *God Made Everything—Just Right!*

God made the sky.
He made it . . . JUST RIGHT!
He made the moon,
 the clouds,
 the stars,
 the sun,
 the planets.
God made the sky.
He made it . . . JUST RIGHT!

God made the land.
He made it . . . JUST RIGHT!
He made the grass,
the rocks,
the hills,
the mountains,
the deserts.
God made the land.
He made it . . . JUST RIGHT!

God made the water.
He made it . . . JUST RIGHT!
He made the oceans,
the rivers,
the lakes,
the brooks
the rain.
God made the water.
He made it . . . JUST RIGHT!

God made the fish.
He made them . . . JUST RIGHT!
He made the salmon,
the tuna,
the cod,
the trout,
the shark.
God made the fish.
He made them . . . JUST RIGHT!

God made the animals.
He made them . . .
JUST RIGHT!
He made the cow,
the horse,
the dog,
the cat,
the lamb.
God made the animals.
He made them . . .
JUST RIGHT!

God made the birds.
He made them . . . JUST RIGHT!
He made the sparrow,
the robin,
the sea gull,
the dove,
the eagle.
God made the birds.
He made them . . . JUST RIGHT!

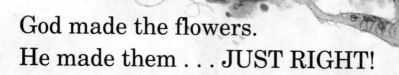

God made the flowers.
He made them . . . JUST RIGHT!

He made the lily,
    the daisy,
    the rose,
    the tulip,
    the pansy.
God made the flowers.
He made them . . . JUST RIGHT!

God made the trees.
He made them . . . JUST RIGHT!
He made the fir tree,
the fig tree,
the pine tree,
the palm tree,
the oak tree.
God made the trees.
He made them . . . JUST RIGHT!

God made you.
He made you . . . JUST RIGHT!
God made your eyes,
your nose,
your mouth,
your arms,
your legs.
God made you.
He made you . . . JUST RIGHT!

God made everything!
He made the sky,
    the land,
    the water,
    the fish,
    the animals,
    the birds,
    the flowers,
    the trees.
And God made you.
God made everything . . .
    JUST RIGHT!

In the beginning God created
the heaven and the earth.

Genesis 1:1

What else did God create
. . . JUST RIGHT?

SEEDLINGS

BOOKS TO GROW ON